Keeping up with Grandpa

JANET BOTTIN

Illustrated by Philip Norman

Scripture Union

By the same author:
Pins and Needles
Amy Peppertree

© Janet Bottin 1999
First published 1999
Reprinted 2002

Scripture Union, 207–209 Queensway, Bletchley, Milton Keynes,
MK2 2EB, England.
Email: info@scriptureunion.org.uk
Website: www.scriptureunion.org.uk

ISBN 1 85999 291 9

British Library Cataloguing-in-Publication Data.
A catalogue record of this book is available from the British Library.

Cover design by Ian Butterworth.
Illustrations by Philip Norman.

Printed and bound in Great Britain by
Creative Print and Design (Wales), Ebbw Vale.

Scripture Union is an international Christian charity working with
churches in more than 130 countries, providing resources to bring the
good news about Jesus Christ to children, young people and families
and to encourage them to develop spiritually through the Bible and
prayer.

As well as our network of volunteers, staff and associates who run
holidays, church-based events and school Christian groups, we
produce a wide range of publications and support those who use our
resources through training programmes.

Contents

This book is dedicated to
"all" my grandchildren
and all the generations to follow...
with infinite love.

Chapter one

Camping Out

"Thank you God for my birthday, and for my new tent, and for making today *so brilliant*," prayed Thomas.

"Amen," said Mum and Grandpa.

"Good-night," said Mum, "Sleep tight."

Mum climbed out of the tent.

Z-Z-Z-Z-Z-Z-ZIP!... down went the tent zip.

"Good-night!" called Thomas and Grandpa.

Mum's footsteps went away.

The house door opened, then closed.

"Grandpa," said Thomas.

"Yesh," answered Grandpa.

"It's getting dark," said Thomas.

"Of coursh, Thomash. It'sh night-time," said Grandpa.

"Why are you talking funny?" asked Thomas.

"I alwaysh take my teeth out at night-time," said Grandpa, "Good-night, Thomash."

"I can hardly see you," said Thomas.

"Thatsh all right," said Grandpa. "You KNOW I'm here. We can't shee God *at all* – but we know HE'SH here. "Good-night, Thomash."

"Grandpa! What's THAT NOISE?" cried Thomas.

"Oh, dear. Wash I shnoring? Shorry, Thomash," said Grandpa.

"It wasn't you. It was OUTSIDE the tent," said Thomas. "There it goes again! There's SOMETHING OUT THERE!"

"There are lotsh of thingsh out there," yawned Grandpa. "Good-night, Thomash."

"I want to go back to the house!" yelled Thomas. "I don't like this tent any more!"

"Why?" asked Grandpa.

"'Cause there are *lots of things* out there!" wailed Thomas.

"Well, sho there are," said Grandpa. "There'sh lotsh of thingsh out there in the daytime, too."

"But I can SEE things in the daytime," cried Thomas. "I *know* what they are!"

Grandpa switched on his torch. It was a big torch with a very bright light. "Let'sh go and eshplore!" he said. "Jusht wait till I pop my teeth in. There! Come along, Thomas."

Thomas didn't want to go. He didn't want to stay alone in the tent, either.

Z-Z-Z-Z-Z-Z-ZIP!... up went the tent zip.

Thomas held tight to Grandpa's hand as they climbed out.

"Grandpa! There's that NOISE!" he shrieked.

Grandpa shone his torch towards the noise.

A hedgehog scrabbling among the leaves blinked in the bright light.

"It's searching for grubs," said Grandpa.

Something went CRUNCH beneath Thomas's feet.

"Oh, OH," he screamed.

Grandpa shone his torch on the ground.

"Oh, dear," he said. "You trod on a snail. Look – there's another one. See the silvery trail it leaves behind as it slides along on its one big foot?"

"Grandpa, WHAT'S that funny SHAPE?" yelled Thomas.

Grandpa's torch shone on the shape.

"It's a blackcurrant bush," he said.

SUDDENLY... there was a loud eerie S-C-R-E-E-C-H.

Thomas stared into the darkness. Four bright lights gleamed back!

"Eeeeeeeee," screamed Thomas, "MARTIANS!"

"Puss, puss. Come here, Minnie," called Grandpa.

Two of the bright lights sped towards Grandpa.

"Minnie was just warning another cat to keep out of our garden. Cats' eyes shine in the dark," explained Grandpa.

"Hello, Minnie Martian!"

Thomas giggled. He stroked Minnie. Minnie p-u-r-r-r-r-e-d.

Thomas felt happy. He gazed up at the twinkling sky.

"God made night-time *brilliant*, too, Grandpa," he said. "Can you and I and Minnie go back to my tent now, and sleep?"

"An *excellent* idea!" yawned Grandpa.

Chapter two

The Biggest Noise

"Thomas! Thomas!" called Thomas's Mum. "I need you, please. Help me get the washing in. Quick!"

Thomas followed Mum's rushing feet down to the clothes-line.

Mum started snatching clothes off the line.

She was in such a hurry, she was scattering pegs all over the lawn.

Thomas chased after the pegs, and put them in the peg-basket.

"There's bad weather coming," said Mum. "I don't like the look of those dark clouds."

"I don't like the look of them, either," said Thomas. "They're black and grumpy – it looks like the sky is frowning. I think I'll go inside again."

"Help me carry the basket of clothes in first, please," said Mum.

Thomas took hold of one end of the clothes basket. Mum took the other end.

Suddenly a bright light flashed in the sky, then went out. It was as if someone had flicked a giant switch on and off again.

"HURRY!" yelled Mum.

"I AM HURRYING!" answered Thomas.

Thomas and Mum rushed with the clothes basket over the lawn and up the back steps.

"GRUMPETY – GRRRRUMP," snarled the grumpy clouds.

"Thumpety-*thump*," went Thomas's heart.

Grandpa helped lift the basket through the doorway into the kitchen.

Just in time...

DOWN came the rain – such a different rain! This wasn't the soft, light, fun sort of rain that Thomas liked to watch and walk in and play in... It was a loud, heavy, fierce rain as if the black clouds were throwing it down as hard as they could!

Then FLASH! went the bright light again.

"GRRRR!" growled the angry sky.

"Oooooooo!" screamed Thomas.

"Yippeee!" cheered Grandpa.

Thomas stopped screaming.

He stared at Grandpa.

The storm was *SCAREY.*

WHY was Grandpa cheering?

"Yahoooo!" cheered Grandpa again. "Quick, Thomas! Let's get into the pots and pans!"

Thomas's eyes opened wider.

"What did Grandpa *mean*? How could they *fit* in the pots and pans?"

"Thomash!" called Grandpa.

Grandpa was upside-down with his head inside the pot cupboard and his voice sounded like his mouth was full of mashed potato...

"Get ush shome lidsh and shpoonsh pleash, Thomash," he mumbled.

Thomas fetched some lids and spoons.

Grandpa put the pots and pans on the kitchen table.

Thomas put the lids and spoons beside the pots and pans.

"Now we're ready!" said Grandpa, smiling.

"Ready for *what*?" asked Thomas, staring.

"Ready to make A JOYFUL NOISE!" said Grandpa. "The lightning and thunder are caused by electrical power in the sky. The GREATEST POWER of all is our God! And he loves us! That's something to be REALLY glad about! Every time the sky makes an angry, bad sound, we're going to make a BIGGER, *glad* sound! Okay, Thomas?"

"Okay!" said Thomas.

He picked up two spoons and stood by the pots and pans.

This was going to be *FUN*.

FLASH! went the lightning.

"Ready?" asked Grandpa, with a lid in each hand and a grin on his face.

The sky began to rumble.

"NOW!" yelled Grandpa.

"Yahoooo! Woopeeee!" cheered Grandpa, clanging his lids.

"Yahoooo! Yippeeee!" cheered Thomas, banging his pots.

Thomas and Grandpa cheered and laughed and clanged and banged and danced and pranced till – finally – the storm was over.

"We made the *biggest* NOISE, Grandpa!" said Thomas. "I couldn't even *hear* the thunder!"

Grandpa smiled, "We've got a reason to make a big noise!" he said. "God's love for us is bigger than *anything* we may be afraid of!"

Chapter three

Super-Thomas

"It's a beautiful day," said Mum. "Go and play out on the lawn, Thomas. But put some shoes on first! There are –"

Thomas didn't wait to hear the rest.

He didn't wait to put his shoes on, either.

He ran out onto the lawn in his bare feet.

He jumped up and down in his bare feet.

He ran round and round in his bare feet.

Grandpa was weeding the garden.

"Thomas!" he called. "You'd better go and put some shoes on. There are –"

Thomas didn't want to hear the rest.

"I'm a SUPERMAN," he yelled. Supermen don't need shoes! Watch me fly."

Super Thomas spread out his arms and ran and jumped all over the soft, springy grass in his bare feet!

Up, down, up, down, "OwwWWWWW!" shrieked Super-Thomas.

"MUM! GRANDPA!" he screamed. "OWWWWWWW!"

Mum and Grandpa both rushed to help.

"It BIT me!" wailed Thomas.

"What bit you?" asked Grandpa. "Where?"

"A *bee*," sobbed Thomas. "*Here*." He pointed to his foot.

Grandpa took hold of Thomas's foot. "*FLICK!*" he went.

"There. The bee sting's gone, Thomas."

Mum had some ointment ready.

"This will stop it hurting," she said. "Thomas, *why weren't you wearing shoes*? I *told* you there were lots of bees about!"

"I told you, too," said Grandpa.

"I didn't hear," sobbed Thomas.

"You didn't WAIT to hear!" said Mum.

"You didn't WANT to hear!" said Grandpa.

"I was being a Superman," whimpered Thomas.

"A REAL Superman would use his supersense," said Grandpa. "He would listen when his Supermum and Supergrandpa warn him how to protect himself from danger!"

"It was the *bee's* fault!" cried Thomas. "I hate, hate, HATE BEES! Why did God make bees with stings?"

"God gave the bees stings so they could protect themselves from danger," said Grandpa.

"It wasn't the bee's fault you got stung, Thomas – it was saving itself from being squashed beneath your foot!"

"Oh," said Thomas. He stopped crying, and started thinking...

"Why did God only give stings to the bees?" he asked.

"Some other insects have stings, too," said Grandpa. "God gave animals lots of different ways to protect themselves. Do you know what hedgehogs have for protection, Thomas?"

"Um... PRICKLES!" cried Thomas.

"Do you know what a stick insect can do so it can't be seen?" asked Grandpa.

"Change colour!" answered Thomas.

"How does a skunk protect itself?" asked Grandpa.

"It *SMELLS*!" answered Thomas, holding his nose. "But Grandpa, what did God give US to protect ourselves?"

"I told you before," said Grandpa. "God made us *SUPERSPECIAL!* He gave us *supersense* to protect ourselves. Tell me, Thomas, why shouldn't you play with matches?"

"They could start a fire," said Thomas.

"What should you do when crossing roads?" asked Grandpa.

"Look both ways and use a crossing," answered Thomas.

"And, what have you learnt about playing outside when there are bees about?" said Grandpa.

"I should wear shoes," answered Thomas.

"*NOW* you're using your *supersense*, Supersensible Thomas!" smiled Grandpa.

Chapter four

No Teeth

"I don't want to go to the dentist!" cried Thomas.

"I'm NOT GOING!"

"She's a very nice lady," said Mum, "She only wants to look in your mouth and check your teeth."

"I won't let her!" yelled Thomas. "I won't open my mouth!"

"If you don't look after your teeth now, you could end up having NO TEETH later," said Mum.

"I don't care," said Thomas.

Grandpa came into the room.

"Wash all the noish about, Thomash?" he said.

Mum and Thomas both stared at Grandpa.

"Grandpa, why are you talking funny?" asked Thomas.

"I *sheem* to have losht my falsh teeth," said Grandpa.

"Lost your false teeth!" cried Mum. "Oh dear. That's sad."

"Thatsh *very shad*," said Grandpa. "I shound shtupid and I look shilly."

It was true – Grandpa didn't only *sound* funny – his cheeks had gone in as if he was sucking hard on a big lolly.

Thomas tried hard not to stare at Grandpa.

"I'll help you look for your teeth, Grandpa," he said.

"Thatsh very kind of you, Thomash," said Grandpa. "Letsh begin with the bathroom..."

They searched in the bathroom.
They searched in the bedrooms.
They searched in the sitting-room.
They searched in the garage.
They searched in the car.
They searched in the garden.
Thomas even looked in the dog's kennel!
But he couldn't find Grandpa's teeth *anywhere*.

"Come and have lunch," said Mum. "You can look again after lunch. Will you say grace please, Grandpa?"

"Thank you God for thish good food," prayed Grandpa, "Thank you for our good health and thank you *shpeshly* for Thomash's good teeth."

Thomas looked at his plate.

He had crunchy carrot sticks, crunchy celery, crunchy potato crisps, a munchy muesli bar, a crunchy cookie and a big crunchy apple! Yum! He started crunching.

After a while Thomas looked at Grandpa.

Grandpa wasn't crunching.

Grandpa wasn't eating at all.

Grandpa was just sitting in his chair looking sad...

"What's the matter Grandpa?" asked Thomas. "It's yummy!"

"I can shee that," said Grandpa. "But I can't eat it, Thomash."

"Would you like some soup, Grandpa?" asked Mum. "You could eat that without teeth."

"Yesh pleash," said Grandpa.

Mum brought Grandpa some soup.

Grandpa lifted a spoonful of soup up to his mouth.

"Slurrrrp," he went, and tried to suck the soup off his spoon.

Some of the soup dribbled down his chin.

"I'm shlopping thish shoup," said Grandpa.

"Try drinking it," said Mum. "I'll pour it

into a mug."

"My mug'sh on the kitshen windowshill," said Grandpa.

Mum picked up Grandpa's mug.

"Grandpa!" she cried. "I've found your teeth! You left them in your mug!"

"Oh, sho I did!" cried Grandpa. "How shilly of me. I'm sho happy you found them. Ish not funny trying to do thingsh without teeth!"

Grandpa popped his teeth into his mouth again.

He smiled.

He looked like Grandpa again.

He sounded like Grandpa again.

"Now Thomas," he said, "What was all that noise about I heard before?"

"Oh, nothing really, Grandpa," said Thomas. "I'm going to visit the dentist this afternoon to have my teeth checked."

"That's very wise of you," said Grandpa. "God expects us to use our brains to take care of our bodies. When we look after things well, they last a lot longer..."

"I'm going to look after my teeth VERY well!" said Thomas.

Chapter five

New Adventures

"Hurry up, Thomas! What's taking SO long? Brush those teeth faster," called Mum.

"I've juzzt got to zzpit out the toothpazzte," slurped Thomas.

"ZZPIT FAST!" called Mum, "And get out here, QUICKLY."

Thomas put down his toothbrush, s-l-o-w-l-y...

He didn't want to leave the bathroom. The bathroom was a small, safe place.

Today Mum was taking him to a strange, new place – a big, busy place where Thomas would have to meet new people and do new things...

Slowly he shuffled to the door.

His legs felt tired. His feet were heavy to lift.

"Well," smiled Mum, "You're ready at

last! Now, how about a big bright smile so I can inspect those gleaming white teeth?"

"CHEESE," grinned Grandpa, popping his head around the corner.

"Beautiful, Grandpa," laughed Mum, "But I was really meaning Thomas!"

"I can't smile," mumbled Thomas. "My face won't stretch. And I can't walk, either. My feet and legs won't move. I think that I should stay at home."

"Stay HOME?" cried Grandpa. "Miss your first day at school? Starting school is a new adventure! *Every time* we start something new, it's the beginning of an adventure. I'm *really* looking forward to starting school today and beginning MY new adventure!"

"Grandpas don't go to SCHOOL!" gasped Thomas.

Sometimes they do," smiled Grandpa. "Your school wanted grandparents to read to the children, so I telephoned and they're expecting me there today. I'M going to be a new school-boy, too!"

"You're a bit old to be a new school-boy, Grandpa!" chuckled Mum.

Thomas giggled.

"Ah," said Grandpa, "That's good – your face can stretch again! Do you think your feet might be able to move, too? Let's find out. Put on that new school-bag and I'll race you to the car..."

Mum drove Thomas and Grandpa to the school.

"This way," Mum said, leading them up some steps to the school office. "We have to enrol you first, and find out which rooms you'll be in."

27

Mum talked to a man in the office.

"Grandpa, can't you and I be in the SAME room?" begged Thomas.

"That wouldn't be nearly as much fun," said Grandpa. "We each need to have our very own new adventure, so we can tell each other about it afterwards. God made everyone different, Thomas, and he plans special adventures for every person. This will be your VERY OWN SPECIAL ADVENTURE. You won't be alone, you know."

"I know," said Thomas. "Jesus will be with me."

Two teachers walked into the room.

"Which of you is my new school-boy?" asked one, smiling.

"I am," said Thomas.

The other teacher smiled at Grandpa.

"Then you must be my new Grandpa," she said.

"I sure am," answered Grandpa.

"And I'm Thomas's mum," said Mum. "How do you do?"

Then everyone shook everyone else's hands.

"Have some GREAT new adventures, you two," said Mum, hugging Thomas and Grandpa.

Thomas's teacher took his hand.

"This way to ADVENTURE-LAND, Thomas," she smiled.

"Happy adventures, Thomas!" called Grandpa.

"You, too, Grandpa!" called Thomas.

Chapter six

Enough to go around

"Tell us THE NEWS!" begged Mum, before Uncle Tim had hardly stepped through the door.

"Our baby was born this morning – a beautiful little daughter," beamed Uncle Tim, proudly.

Then everyone began talking at once.

After a while Grandpa asked, "But... WHERE'S your OTHER beautiful daughter?"

"She's here," said Uncle Tim, reaching behind him and pulling forward a little girl with her thumb in her mouth. "She's very tired, and she's not quite sure how she feels about having to share me and her mum with a new little sister."

Thomas stared. He couldn't remember meeting his cousin before. She didn't look much fun to play with.

"I've got a cosy bed all ready for a tired little girl," Mum smiled.

"Great!" said Uncle Tim. "Come along, Keri. I'll tuck you in before I drive back home."

"Wanna go home, too," wailed Keri.

"You'll have a great holiday here, playing with Thomas," said Uncle Tim.

"Don't wanna holiday. Don't wanna play with Thomas. Don't wanna go to bed," yelled Keri.

"I guess you *don't want* the SURPRISE in your bed, either," said Grandpa.

"W-WHAT surprise?" asked Keri.

"Is there a surprise in *my* bed, too?" asked Thomas.

"No, Thomas," answered Grandpa.

"Why can't *I* have a surprise?" grumbled Thomas.

"You might, when it's the right time for you to have one," said Grandpa.

"It's NOT FAIR," moaned Thomas.

"I think I'll go to bed now," said Keri.

"Good girl," said Uncle Tim.

Next morning Keri arrived at breakfast holding a box.

She wouldn't let Thomas see inside.

Thomas decided he didn't like Keri.

After breakfast Keri hid her secret box.

Thomas went out and played on the swing.

Keri came outside.

"Can I have a turn?" she asked.

Thomas pretended not to hear.

Keri kept on asking.

Thomas kept on pretending.

Then Grandpa came outside.

"Grandpa! Thomas won't give me a turn!" yelled Keri.

"Grandpa! Keri won't show me her stupid surprise!" shouted Thomas.

"It's NOT a *stupid* surprise!" cried Keri.

"Show it, then," bawled Thomas.

"Don't have to!" yelled Keri.

Then Mum heard the noise and came outside.

"Do you think I should take these children to visit my friend's farm?" Grandpa asked her.

"The sooner the better, I'd say," Mum replied. "I've never forgotten the time you took Tim and me!"

Thomas and Keri forgot about squabbling. They rushed to get ready...

Grandpa drove them into the country.

"We're here!" he said, stopping the car.

"WHAT'S THAT *SMELL*?" asked Keri.

"Pigs," grinned Grandpa.

Grandpa's friend came to meet them.

"So, you've come to see my piglets!" he said, winking at Grandpa. "Follow me."

"WHAT'S THAT *NOISE*?" asked Thomas.

"It's the piglets squabbling," said Grandpa, "Watch! God made the sow with lots of teats and enough milk to go around them all – just like God's love is enough for everyone everywhere, all around the world! But look how the piglets push and climb over each other and won't give others a turn..."

"They're GREEDY," cried Keri.

"They should SHARE," said Thomas.

"EXACTLY!" grinned Grandpa.

"Keri, *you* can have first turn on the swing when we get home," offered Thomas.

"Thanks, Thomas," smiled Keri. "While I'm swinging, *you* can play with the things in my box!"

Chapter seven

Upside-down

"Look Thomas – look at the upside-down ducks," giggled Keri.

Thomas looked.

He saw three ducks' tails bobbing about in the water. The ducks' heads were all *under* the water!

"What are they doing?" Thomas asked.

"They're hunting for food," answered Grandpa.

"What sort of food?" asked Keri.

"Crunchy bugs and juicy grubs," grinned Grandpa.

"YUK!" Thomas and Keri pulled faces.

"I'm glad we brought some bread with us," said Keri. "At least *today* the poor ducks can have something nice."

"Ducks think bugs and grubs are nice," said Grandpa. "They eat them because they LIKE them!"

"I'm glad I'm not a duck!" shuddered Keri, as she divided the bread between her and Thomas.

Thomas broke his bread into big pieces and threw them as far as he could into the lake.

The ducks rushed and fought to get there first.

"Learn to SHARE!" Thomas called to them.

Soon his bread was all used up.

Keri was breaking hers into tiny pieces and feeding ducks at the edge of the lake.

"Here, Thomas – have some of *my* bread," she said. "Let's throw it on the grass and see if the ducks will come close to us."

The ducks weren't afraid at all.

They crowded around the children.

One even walked over Thomas's shoe.

"Our bread's all gone," said Keri.

The ducks didn't believe her.

"Quack! Quack!" they said, crowding closer.

"Our time's all gone, too – we have to leave," said Grandpa. "I'll race you to the car!"

The ducks raced to the car after them.

Thomas and Keri jumped in the back.

One of the ducks jumped in too! Keri and Thomas didn't tell Grandpa.

Grandpa climbed in the front and drove off. He didn't see the duck!

"Are you hungry?" Grandpa asked. "Shall we stop for ice-creams, or would you rather have a beetle?"

"Quack! Quack!" answered the stowaway duck.

"Did I hear you children say you wanted BEETLES?" gasped Grandpa.

"Quack! Quack!" said the duck again.

"Have my grandchildren turned into DUCKS?" cried Grandpa.

Keri and Thomas burst into giggles.

Grandpa stopped the car and peered in the back.

"Ah-hah! A STOWAWAY," he cried. "So YOU'RE the one that wants beetles!"

"Quack! Quack!" answered the duck.

"Can we keep it, Grandpa?" asked Thomas.

"*Please*, Grandpa," begged Keri.

"God made ducks to live in the water," said Grandpa. "He gave them webbed feet for paddles, and oil to waterproof their feathers and special beaks for catching and eating their food. Our clever God made creatures in special ways to suit special places. The duck wouldn't be happy living in our house. Would *you* be happy living in his lake?"

"No WAY!" cried Thomas and Keri.

"It would make everything back-to-front," said Thomas.

"And upside-down!" added Keri.

"We should take him back," said Thomas.

"Then he can have his beetle," added Keri.

"Quack! Quack!" said the duck.

"A good idea," said Grandpa. "You could have one too – or would you rather have ice-creams?"

"ICE-CREAMS, *PLEASE*, Grandpa!" shouted Thomas and Keri.

Chapter eight

Nobody Answered

*Suggestion for story-tellers: cup your hand to your ear as a signal for your audience to join in with the repeated phrase – *Nobody answered...

Mum had gone out. Grandpa was looking after Thomas and Keri. He said prayers with them, dimmed their light, then went into the kitchen to wash the dishes.

"Grandpa! *We want a story*!" Thomas called.

Rattle, rattle went the dishes.

Nobody answered.

"GRANDPA! TELL US A STORY!" shouted Keri.

Still –

Nobody answered.

"Grandpa! Grandpa! WE WANT A STORY!" yelled Thomas and Keri together.

But –

Nobody answered.

Then Grandpa appeared in the doorway.

"Goodnight, children. Sweet dreams," he said. Then he went back to the kitchen.

"GRANDPA!" yelled Thomas. "What about our *STORY?*"

Nobody answered.

"I don't think he heard you," said Keri. "Let's try together."

So Thomas and Keri started chanting, getting louder and *louder...*

"WE WANT A STORY!
WE WANT A STORY!
WE WANT A STORY!"

But –

Nobody answered.

"Do you think Grandpa's gone *deaf*?" Thomas asked Keri.

"My mum goes deaf sometimes," said Keri. "She says there's a special word that helps her to hear."

"What is it?" asked Thomas.

"It's *please*," replied Keri.

"Let's try it," said Thomas.

"PLEASE, Grandpa, PLEASE will you tell us a story, *PLEASE*?" called Thomas and Keri.

Grandpa arrived AT ONCE.

"Of *course* I'll tell you a story," he said. "How could I refuse *three pleases*?

Jesus is so happy when we speak to each other kindly and ask for things politely."

He sat down and started his story –

"Benjamin Bear jumped out of bed.
'Honey for breakfast! Hurrah,' he said.
'Honey in porridge. Honey on toast.
Honey's the food that I love most!
Pass me the honey!'
'I'm sorry, Benjamin,' said Robert Rabbit.
'The cupboard is bare – there's no honey there.'

Benjamin Bear called to the bees,
'Bees! Bees! *Make me some honey*!'
'We're sorry, Benjamin,' said the bees,
'the flowers won't bloom. We can't make honey.'
Benjamin Bear called to the flowers,
'Flowers! Flowers! *Bloom for the bees*, so that the bees can *make me some honey*!'
'We're sorry, Benjamin,' said the flowers,
'It's such a shame, but the clouds won't rain.
We need a shower to help us flower.'
So Benjamin Bear called to the clouds,
'Clouds! Clouds! *Rain for the flowers*, so that the flowers can bloom for the bees so that the bees can *make me some honey*!'
'We're sorry, Benjamin,' said the clouds.
'We cannot rain unless you say *"PLEASE."*
Bears who are rude deserve no food.'
Benjamin Bear drooped his head, and said, 'PLEASE, clouds, rain for the flowers.
PLEASE, flowers, bloom for the bees.
PLEASE, bees, make me some honey.
Honey, you know, is my favourite food,
I'm VERY sorry that I was rude.'
Then – the clouds began raining, the flowers began blooming and the bees

began busily making honey.

Now when Benjamin comes downstairs
'Honey for breakfast! Hurrah!' he says.
'Honey in porridge. Honey on toast.
Honey's the food that I love most!
PLEASE pass me the honey.'

Benjamin learnt that PLEASE is a word
that helps things happen!

Did you like that story, children?" asked
Grandpa.

But –

Keri and Thomas had fallen asleep and –
*Nobody answered...

Chapter nine

Lost and Found

The ice-cream van music faded away...

"Mum, *why* couldn't we have money for ice-creams?" grumbled Thomas.

"You don't have to have ice-creams *every time* the van comes around!" answered Mum.

"But we *wanted* one," whined Thomas.

Thomas and Keri wandered outside to play.

"Thomas, *I* know how we can get money for ice-creams," said Keri.

"*HOW*?" asked Thomas.

"From *teeth*," answered Keri. "My friend who's six had a wobbly tooth. It came out. She put it under her pillow and she said it turned into money."

"Let's feel our teeth!" said Thomas.

Keri and Thomas put their fingers into their mouths and tested all their teeth – but neither of them found any that wobbled.

"Well – *that* won't work!" sighed Thomas.

That night Thomas had to get up to use the toilet.

On the bathroom shelf he saw a mug. *Inside* the mug were LOTS OF TEETH – Grandpa's "Take-out" teeth!

Thomas *TOOK* them!

He scampered back to bed and hid them under his pillow...

Next morning Thomas peeked under his pillow expecting to find LOTS OF MONEY.

But all he saw was – Grandpa's teeth...

"Perhaps they need to stay there longer," Thomas thought.

So he slid the teeth back under his pillow, and – *left them there*...

All that day Grandpa looked puzzled and talked funny.

"I jusht don't undershtand where my teeth have gone," he kept saying, "I'm absholutely shertain I put them in my mug lasht night. It'sh a real myshtery..."

Thomas felt sorry for Grandpa, especially at meal-times. Watching Grandpa trying to eat made Thomas feel mean and bad.

But getting ice-cream money seemed more important.

All day Thomas and Keri kept checking under Thomas's pillow.

They even tried the teeth under Keri's pillow.

But Grandpa's teeth still stayed ... *just Grandpa's teeth*.

"Perhaps it doesn't work with "Take-out" teeth," Thomas sighed. "Come on, Keri – we'd better put them back."

They crept through the dining-room.

Nobody was around.

There was a bowl of chocolate mousse on the bench.

Keri dipped a finger in and licked it.

"*Yum,*" she said.

Thomas dipped a finger in too, and... *dropped Grandpa's teeth*!

The teeth *SANK* into the mousse – *and* – *DISAPPEARED*!

"Someone's coming!" cried Thomas, and he and Keri disappeared *quickly* too!

At meal-time Keri said, "I don't want any mousse, thank you, Auntie."

"I don't either," said Thomas.

"Well... *THAT'S* A SURPRISE!" said Mum.

"*I do*, pleashe," said Grandpa, "It'sh eashy to eat mousshe without teeth."

He dipped his spoon into the chocolate mousse.

"What'sh THISH?" he cried, "My *TEETH*!"

Grandpa looked at Thomas and Keri.

"Ish there shomething shomebody should tell me?" he asked.

Thomas went pink.

"I took your teeth, Grandpa," he said.

Then he told the whole story.

"Well, Thomas, what did you *get* from taking something that wasn't yours... *nice-tasting ice-creams?*" asked Grandpa.

"No," answered Thomas, "Bad, sad feelings. I'm *really sorry*, Grandpa."

"Sorry, Grandpa," echoed Keri.

"I forgive you," said Grandpa. "But isn't there Someone Else you should be saying sorry to?"

"Sorry, Jesus," prayed Thomas and Keri.

Thomas felt happiness like warm sunshine chasing his gloomy feelings away.

"Thank you for forgiving me, Jesus," he whispered.

49

Chapter ten

Once Upon a Rock

Suggestion for story-tellers: children could create a *"swishing"* background to accompany the words *"Swishh... swashh... washh..."* by rubbing the palms of their hands together.

Thomas and Keri and Grandpa and Mum all paddled at the water's edge.

Swishh... swashh... washh.... the little waves washed up on the sand, then hurried back to the sea.

"Let's jump the next wave," called Grandpa. "Everyone hold hands. Are you all ready?"

Swishh... swashh... washh... the little waves came rolling towards them.

"JUMP!" yelled Thomas.

Grandpa jumped.

Mum jumped.

Keri jumped.

Thomas jumped – but a bit too late.

SPLASH... went the waves against his legs.

"They caught you, Thomas!" giggled Keri.

"Let's make castles, now," said Thomas. He ran up the beach to his bucket and spade and started digging in the damp sand.

"There's a bucket and spade for you, too, Keri!" he called.

Keri looked up and down the beach, searching for just the right place for a castle...

Then, she saw it!

"I won't need a bucket and spade!" she replied.

Thomas looked puzzled.

"My castle's already been made," explained Keri, and she ran down the beach towards a huge rock.

"*That's* not a sandcastle!" Thomas shouted.

"No – it's a *ROCK CASTLE!*" Keri called back.

Thomas worked hard, building a *magnificent* sandcastle. There was a turret at each corner, a moat with a driftwood drawbridge, and a flag made from a stick and a scrap of sea-weed.

Meanwhile, Keri collected shells and sea-weed and sea-side flowers, and decorated her special rock.

They'd both been too busy to notice the little waves creeping higher and higher up the beach – then, *SUDDENLY* –

Swishh... swashh... washh.... a little wave sneaked over the sand and filled up the moat around Thomas's sandcastle.

"STOP! KEEP AWAY! GO BACK!" cried Thomas.

But more little waves kept rolling in.

Swishh... swashh... washh.... they washed against Thomas's sandcastle.

Swishh... swashh... washh.... they washed pieces off Thomas's sandcastle.

Swishh... swashh... washh.... they washed *into* Thomas's sandcastle and *over* Thomas's sandcastle, until Thomas's sandcastle was **all washed away!**

Swishh... swashh... washh.... the little waves washed around and splashed against Keri's rock-castle, but they COULDN'T wash *that* away!

Keri sat on her rock and sang...

"Swish-swash sea

Swish-swash sea

You *won't* break my rock

And you can't catch me!"

"Why did my sandcastle wash away" wailed Thomas. "I wanted it to stay for EVER. Keri still has *her* castle!"

"Your two castles remind me of a story Jesus told about two people who chose different places to build their houses, just like you two," said Grandpa. "One built his house on the sand, like Thomas. The other built his on a rock, like Keri. Then a great rainstorm came. Guess which house got washed away?"

"The one on the sand," sighed Thomas.

"Yes," smiled Grandpa. "But the house on the rock *held together*. A rock won't wash away. Jesus said *he's* like a rock! When we ask him to be our friend, he's a FRIEND FOR EVER."

"Climb up on my rock. Thomas," called Keri. "Let's make up songs!"

Thomas and Keri sat on the rock-castle and sang...

"Swish-swash waves,
Splish-splosh weather,
Jesus is our FRIEND
For ever *and* EVER!"

Chapter eleven

Playing the Game

"I wish Keri could be a ROCK," sighed Thomas.

"What a *strange* wish!" gasped Mum.

"A rock doesn't go away," explained Thomas. "Like Jesus – he's *always* here, and he'll *always* be my friend."

"Oh, I see," said Mum. "I know you've enjoyed Keri being here, Thomas – but she needs her own family, especially her new little sister. Keri will be able to come for holidays again, and you've *still* got today together... Now, are you both ready to go to the football game? Because Grandpa is!"

"I'll just get my hat!" said Keri.

As they drove to the sports ground Grandpa said, "Instead of *wishing* Keri could stay, Thomas, why not try *thinking* of ways you could keep being friends after she leaves?"

"Um... we could talk on the phone," said Thomas.

"And send things in the post," added Keri.

"Now *that's thinking*!" smiled Grandpa.

At the sports ground they found a seat right next to Mum's friend, Mrs Miranda.

Keri put on her pink frilly sun-hat. Grandpa tied the ribbons under her chin.

"I'm going to cheer for the green team," said Keri.

"I am, too," said Thomas.

"*I* am, *too*," said Grandpa. "An old friend of mine used to play for that team."

The game started.

"*GO, GREEN!*" yelled Thomas and Keri and Grandpa.

By half-time the green team was winning by two goals.

"Did you see how the players shared the ball, and passed it to each other? I know two children who have learnt to play together like that," said Grandpa, "Can those children keep rules like good players do, too? A rule to keep right now, is – '*Stay in your seats.*'"

Grandpa turned to Mrs Miranda.

"Could you please watch the children for a moment?" he said. "I've just glimpsed an old friend in the crowd."

Grandpa hurried away, looking excited.

Keri untied the ribbons on her sun-hat.

"This ribbon's too tight," she said.

Suddenly, a gust of wind flicked the sun-hat off her head, and flew away with it!

"I HAVE to find it!" cried Keri, leaping up.

"Your grandpa said to stay in your seats," Mrs Miranda reminded her.

Keri sat down again.

"My *sunhat*," she sobbed. "I *want it back*!"

"It's coming back!" cried Thomas, "*LOOK!*"

The children both stared.

Keri's pink frilly sun-hat was bobbing about amongst the crowd. It came closer... *and CLOSER... up... the... steps...*

Underneath the sun-hat was... GRANDPA'S HEAD!

"Here, Keri," said Grandpa, "This looks better on you than it does on me!"

"It looked pretty good on you, too, Joe!" laughed a man with Grandpa.

Grandpa thanked Mrs Miranda for minding the children.

Then he handed Thomas and Keri each a bag of pop-corn.

"These are the prizes for two good players who also *keep rules*," he smiled, "And *this* is my old friend, Mr Armstrong. We haven't seen each other for *forty-two years*, but we've kept up our friendship by phone and post."

"Hello, children," smiled Mr Armstrong.

"Wow!" whispered Thomas to Keri, "I'm glad we won't have to wait *THAT* long before we see each other again!"

Chapter twelve

Jack-in-the-box

Thomas stared at his plate.

"I don't feel like eating," he said.

Mum and Grandpa stared at Thomas.

Nothing like THIS had ever happened before!

"Are you missing Keri?" Mum asked Thomas.

"Does missing people make you feel like not eating?" wondered Thomas.

"Sometimes," answered Grandpa. "I didn't feel much like *my* meals for a while without Grandma around to share them with me. I found talking to Jesus helped those lonely feelings go away. Jesus knows all about loneliness – sometimes he felt VERY lonely. Helping other lonely people helped me feel less lonely, too..."

"Did feeling lonely make your head ache, Grandpa?" asked Thomas.

"Sometimes," answered Grandpa.

"Did it make you ITCH?" asked Thomas.

"*ITCH*! I don't think so!" chuckled Grandpa.

"Uh-oh," said Mum.

She hurried over to Thomas.

She lifted his T-shirt and stared at his tummy.

"UH-OH," she said again.

Thomas peered down at his tummy, too.

He saw lots of little red spots.

"Does feeling lonely give people *SPOTS?*" he gasped.

"No," answered Mum, "but CHICKEN-POX does!"

"Chickenpops!" cried Thomas. "Have I got *chickenpops*?"

"You certainly have," said Mum. "They're chickenpopping up all over! No school for you tomorrow – just lots of rest, and lots to drink – and NO SCRATCHING!"

All the next day Thomas had to stay home, indoors.

And the next day...

And the next day...

"Chickenpops are BORING," he moaned. "I WISH Keri were here. I'm LONELY."

Grandpa came in, carrying a box.

"What's *that*?" asked Thomas.

Grandpa smiled.

"This is a special Chickenpox Treasurebox, especially for a child with chickenpox."

"*I'm* a child with chickenpops!" squeaked Thomas excitedly.

"Well, this must be for you, then," said Grandpa, putting the Chickenpox Treasurebox down beside Thomas.

Thomas lifted the lid and reached inside.

"AHHH!" he squealed, "There's something WET in there!"

Then out from the box popped a little head with a licky tongue.

"It's a JACK-in-the-box!" grinned Grandpa.

"It's a pup-in-the-box," laughed Mum.

"Is it for ME?" cried Thomas. "Can I *keep* it? Please, Grandpa! *Please*, Mum!"

"Little Jack needs proper care," said Grandpa. "He'll miss his mother. Can you care for him properly?"

"I can, I CAN," promised Thomas.

"He needs to be taught to behave, too," said Mum. "Will you do that, Thomas?"

"I will, I WILL," promised Thomas, cuddling the puppy.

"Here's his puppy food," said Mum, putting a bowl down on the floor. "He needs that much three times a day..."

"Food, Jack!" said Thomas, sitting the pup beside the bowl.

Jack gobbled hungrily.

"He doesn't need to be taught how to eat!" laughed Grandpa.

Thomas was staring at the carpet.

"Uh-oh," he murmured.

"He needs to be taught the right place to do THAT, though!" said Mum.

"I'll teach him," promised Thomas. "I'll teach him *everything*. And I'll be his best friend, so he won't feel lonely without his mother. I'll love him *all the time*, just like Jesus loves me!"

"Jack's yours, then," smiled Mum and Grandpa.

"Ohhhhh... THANK YOU!" cried Thomas. He could *hardly wait* to write and tell Keri...

Dear Keri

Mum is helping me write this letter to tell you what I got. I got **chickenpox**. **And**...I got **a puppy**! I liked getting Jack, my puppy, best.

Love from Thomas.
